Dexter Chase

A Gay Erotic Romance

Chance *of the* HEART

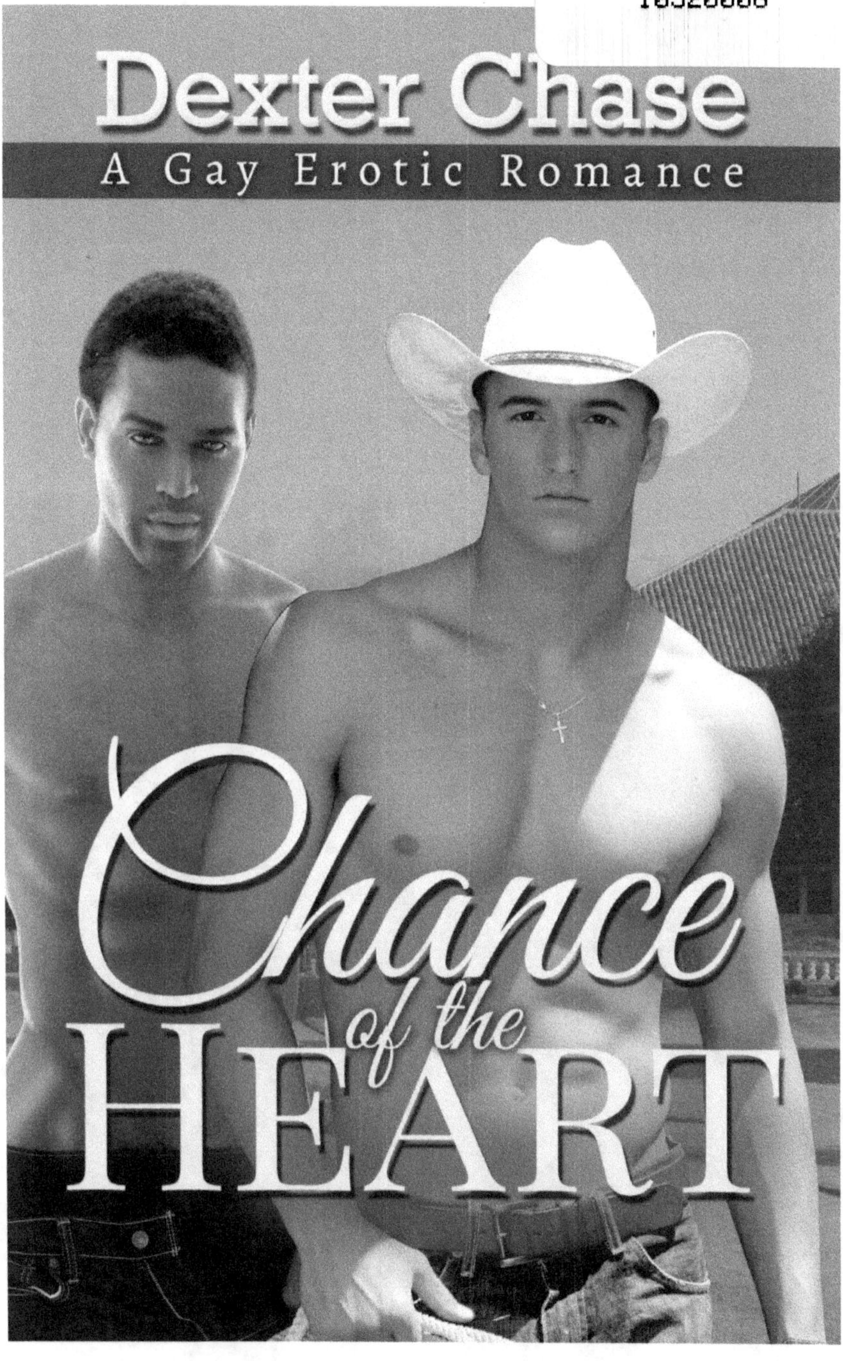

WARNING

This book contains sexually explicit scenes and adult language. It may be considered offensive to some readers. This book is for sale to adults ONLY.

* * * * * * * * * * * * * * * * * * *

Please store your files wisely where they cannot be accessed by underage readers.

Please feel free to send me an email. Just know that these emails are filtered by my publisher. Good news is always welcome.

Dexter Chase - **dexter_chase@awesomeauthors.org**

About the Publisher

4Fun Publishing, a member of **BLVNP Incorporated**, 340 S. Lemon #6200, Walnut CA 91789, info@blvnp.com / legal@blvnp.com

NOTE: Due to the highly emotional reaction of some people to works of erotic fiction, any email sent to the above address that contains foul language or religious references is automatically deleted by our anti-spam software and will not be seen. All other communications are welcome.

DISCLAIMER

Please don't be stupid and kill yourself. This book is a work of FICTION. Do not try any new sexual practice that you find in this book. It is fiction and not to be confused with reality. Neither the author nor the publisher or its associates assume any responsibility for any loss, injury, death or legal consequences resulting from acting on the contents in this book. Every character in this book is over 18 years of age. The author's opinions are not to be construed as the opinions of the publisher. The material in this book is for entertainment purposes ONLY. Enjoy.

Chance of the Heart

A Gay Erotic Romance

By: Dexter Chase

ISBN: 978-1-68030-266-0

Chapter 1

Thomas Langley Sharp III, whenever Tom thought about it he didn't know whether to laugh or cry. Laugh because it was just such an awfully pretentious name, or cry because the loving parents that had given it to him had died the eve of his nineteenth birthday.

Tom now lived with the man that had been his tutor, valet and general Man Friday since his birth. Valerie was a softly spoken French man of small stature, but Tom's father had chosen him because he had all the talents he wanted taught to Tom and despite his small stature he was a master of martial arts and the best bodyguard Tom could ever have wished for. Engaged to this new position at the age of 21, with a brand new degree in literature he kept studying and learning almost full time during Tom's early years.

Tom had never been allowed to slack despite his father's wealth so he was a fine sportsman, excellent equestrian, more than adequate academic and gay. From puberty until he was sixteen he had tried to seduce Valerie, unsuccessfully. Valerie was that rare breed of asexual, no carnal desires at all. The reason for the change in Tom was Daniel, also sixteen and a fellow rider, as good an equestrian as Tom who quickly grew to admire this black boy. Like Tom he had not been gifted with great height or size. Neither of them had managed to exceed five feet nine inches, but their bodies were in complete proportion to their height.

Daniel had left school at sixteen because academics were not his thing and his parents had died that year. He worked as a stable boy at the stables from which they both rode, and quickly became friends.

Their first conversations were very stilted, both conscious of the class gap.

"Hello, my name's Tom, thank you for looking after Eagle for me."

Daniel found it difficult to find words for a reply, stood in front of this very dominant young white.

"Thank you Sir, I'm Daniel, and Mr. Loftus has allocated Eagle to me."

Tom laughed a jolly laugh.

"Oh Daniel, I'm not a, Sir, I'm Tom. Can we be friends?"

Daniel wasn't prepared for this. Most of the owners treated him with disdain. He looked at this new face and saw nothing but joie de vie, (joy of life), in the eyes of this boy who looked about the same age as he was.

"I suppose so, Sir."

A pleading look from Tom made Daniel realise he meant what he said.

"Please Daniel, I don't like, Sir, and I would like us to be friends if you are looking after Eagle for me."

Daniel nodded, "Alright Tom. He is beautiful and I do so love to ride him when he needs exercise."

The horse broke the ice, both boys could talk all day about horses. Tom was building his ability so that he could start taking part in eventing. Daniel said he would love to do that as well if he ever got the chance. That comment set in motion a series of actions from Tom.

The first one was that he found himself at the stable more frequently and often had Daniel take his slot with the trainer. He didn't take long to realise that Daniel was a natural.

The second one was a very quick deepening of their friendship. Daniel soon learnt to relax around Tom and his natural character showed.

The third was that Tom fell in love with this boy.

"Dad."

Tom Sharp II looked up from his paper as his son joined the family for breakfast.

"Yes Thomas, good morning."

Tom grinned, "Sorry Dad, good morning Mother, Father."

The grin could always get a favourable response.

"Now what is so important?"

"My new stable lad rides Eagle a lot, and wants to do eventing the same as me. He doesn't get much chance because the trainers won't teach him and he has no horse. I will need a spare when I start in competition, and it would be good for the horses if they were trained together all the time. If you buy me my second horse now, and pay a higher proportion of Daniel's salary, he could train with me and we could swap horses so that both horses are familiar with our different styles."

Thomas looked hard at his son.

"What's so special about this lad?"

Tom blushed as he replied. "He's black, lives at the stables, so I suppose he is poor. He's the same age as me and a really nice guy. He loves Eagle and looks after him special."

Thomas was aware that Tom was gay, Valerie had done his duty to his employer by informing him after Tom hit puberty. Nothing had been said because Thomas was more interested in who his son was, not what he was. He had done nothing but bring pleasure into the lives of his parents who had become parents quite late in life.

"Mmm, perhaps a black Arab, then you could ride pairs if you were good, and be a contrast."

Tom thought his father was winding him up and blushed.

"I'm serious Tom. We'll look for another horse straight away and I'll come out to the stables to talk about Daniel's contract."

Being buried in kisses by this sixteen year old boy didn't faze Thomas at all. In fact it increased the joy he found in this miniature Sharp.

The next trip Tom made to the stables for training, his father came with him, firstly to have a look at this black boy. It didn't take him many minutes to see how much they liked each other. They never appeared to grow tired of light touches to each other as they spoke and Thomas could see how much care that Daniel took with Eagle.

Daniel nearly jumped out of his skin when Mr. Sharp addressed him.

"Young man, before I talk to Mr. Loftus, would you like to work and train with Tom exclusively? You will have no responsibilities except the care of Eagle and his new mate when we find him. You will have as much access to the trainer as you wish, and ride with Tom always."

Daniel didn't know what to say until Tom slung an arm over his shoulder and spoke.

"This is my Dad, Dan, and all you have to say is yes."

Daniel spluttered out a yes and Thomas turned to walk to the office smiling at the delightful shyness of the young boy.

Mr. Loftus was delighted to accede to Mr. Sharp's wishes. He would get another horse, income for Daniel's keep and extra fees for trainer use during periods when the man might have been sat doing nothing.

On the same day that the new black Arab arrived, Daniel nearly had apoplexy. Valerie and Tom took him down to the riding shop and kitted him out with all new riding gear, boots, jodhpurs, shirts and jackets, helmets, gloves, the list appeared almost endless. At the end, Daniel just broke down and threw himself into Tom's arms, managing a very tearful 'thank you, no one has ever been this nice to me in my life.'

The next big event for both boys was driving lessons. Both boys were more than ready for the practical test on their seventeenth birthdays. Theory had been completed earlier, Tom went with Daniel for his test, sat on tenterhooks until car and examiner returned, and a grinning Daniel rushed into the waiting room waving his pass certificate. Two months later, Daniel performed the same vigil for Tom.

Next surprise for both boys was Thomas sitting them down for a talk.

"I don't think the riding school is the right place for Daniel now that he can drive. If you agree with me Tom, I would like you both to have cars now and Daniel can then drive here when he finishes work every day. I thought the adjoining suite to yours would be suitable. Plenty of stowage space for his riding clothes."

Tom couldn't even begin to control his emotions with that statement. His father was, in the only way he knew how, informing his son that Daniel was now considered family. Result was a very wet shirt as Tom cried out his pleasure all over his father. Daniel meanwhile was too stupefied to say anything for ages.

For Tom, this move was crunch time. He and Daniel had become very tight friends, very touchy feely, but nothing sexual. Tom didn't even know if Daniel was gay. They never talked about girls, or boys come to that. Now they were going to be living in adjoining rooms. Both were en-suite so Tom never got the chance to see Daniel naked, or even partly clothed, but the proximity was painful for Tom whose imagination had them making love all the time.

The next big event was an 'event' where Daniel took the Blue Ribbon on Foxglove, the new black Arab. Tom came second on Eagle and was not at all upset. In the parade ring to receive their prizes, they looked a stunning pair. Tom wore a scarlet jacket with white trousers, white shirt and white silk cravat. His black boots shined to a mirror finish, sat astride his white Arabian. Daniel was dressed head to toe in black except for his white shirt and white silk cravat, sat astride a black Arabian with a coat that shone like gloss. Black and white gloves met in a handshake and no one was in any doubt that Thomas Langley Sharp III was a good sport and delighted to see his stable companion win.

Daniel had always tried to act with decorum around Tom's parents but back at the unsaddling enclosure that went out the window when Thomas and Charlotte Sharp jointly presented him with his own beautifully tooled saddle.

"We hope this will be a constant reminder of your first event win, Daniel, and congratulations from the family, Son."

Daniel just looked at this beautiful piece of equipment and burst into tears. Tom had his friend in a hug before anyone else could move.

"I am so proud of you, Dan. You were brilliant."

Daniel snuffled, trying so hard to regain control, eventually achieving a semblance of it. He looked round at all the cheering riders and grooms that had watched before looking at Thomas and Charlotte.

"I have no words that come close to voicing my thanks, Sir, and Ma'am. I will try so hard to make you as proud of me as you are of Tom."

It was a tearful young man that sat with his friend as they were driven home, having looked after the horses and seen them into the van for transportation back to the stables.

"I think we should all go home and get cleaned up, then up to the stables to give our two boys their reward, and then I'll take you all to dinner."

Thomas realised, that despite the fact that Daniel had been living with them for some time, he had never taken him with them on a family dinner.

Two very distinguished looking teenage boys walked into a luxury restaurant near Windsor, immaculately dressed and oozing good health and self-confidence.

Tom was so proud of Daniel, he looked like he had been born to this life style. The facade crumbled briefly, but not observed by any other diners when they were settled and Thomas spoke.

"Your mother and I have observed with pleasure your burgeoning friendship with Daniel, Tom. So, Daniel, we think it is way past time you ceased to be so formal with us. We would be so proud if you would call us Mum and Dad from now on."

Both boys teared up and went to the next level. Tears streaming down their faces they said almost in unison. "Thank you Mum, Dad, I love you so much."

That changed the tears to laughter and Daniel thought he would never be happier in his life.

From the time that his parents had died to the present time Daniel could hardly believe how his life had changed. From a stable boy living in a basic room above a stable, to the height of luxury and a new reputation as an event rider. The biggest plus to all that was Tom, he was so beautiful and friendly, he could eat him, but putting a move on his only friend could so easily bring his walls tumbling down, but he loved this friend who never had a cross word to say and always a ready smile in his eyes and on his lips.

Tom finished his 'A' Level exams and tried to persuade his father that university wasn't necessary. He was surprised when his father acquiesced.

"Conditions apply. I have been expecting this so Valerie has been taking advanced courses in finance and business management. Provided you undertake these courses seriously I will allow you to remain at home. Slack and I will reverse that decision and you will go to university or I'll sell the horses."

A horrendous thought but Tom agreed the terms. He would not have to leave Dan. Both boys were now eighteen and Tom decided that action needed to be taken to see if Dan would contemplate a gay relationship. The decision was taken out of his hands by an act that he could not have organised better himself.

Just after Christmas of their graduating year the weather turned very cold and the lake on the farm froze, but not too hard. Daniel and Tom were fooling around after changing back into street clothes when they had finished riding. Dan ran out onto the ice and broke through.

Tom ran for the stables and brought rope for rescue. When he had Dan ashore the boy was nearly passing out he was so cold. Tom knew there was a hose attached to a hot/cold water supply at the end of the stables. They ran together straight for that area and Tom made Dan strip naked.

"Put your hands behind your head, I'm going to give you a hot shower."

Tom was almost crying with pleasure watching his friend. The hot water quickly relaxed Daniel and he started to lengthen between his legs. Tom grabbed two large towels and a horse blanket, wrapped Daniel in them and pulled him into a hug.

"Oh Dan. I have never seen a more beautiful human being in my life."

Daniel laughed and just said, "Flatterer."

"No Dan, I mean it and that monster between your legs needs to be worshipped every day."

Tom said that with a laugh. Daniel's reply wasn't humorous though.

"I've never seen you like this Tom, but I know if I did I would want to worship you for the rest of my life."

Both boys looked searchingly into each other's eyes before Tom spoke again.

"I love you Dan, I think I have for a long time. Seeing you naked has made me realise I can't hide it any more. I want to make love to you forever."

Daniel hardly gave Tom time to draw breath before placing his lips over Tom's and kissing him like he meant it. When they parted there was only wonder left in their eyes until Dan broke the spell.

"My feet are cold."

Poor Dan, he was stood on a bare concrete floor. Tom picked him up in his arms and walked him through to the farm house. Not particularly exciting but he found a bedroom and dropped Daniel on to the bed and fell on it beside him.

"I love you so much and I'm going to start at your feet to show you."

That was more than Tom bargained for. He realised Dan's feet had been seriously cold. Warming them took a long time and before continuing his play time he ran to his locker and came back with a very thick pair of Shetland wool socks. He locked the door in case Mr. Loftus came along, and then started what he had wanted to do for nearly two years. He made love to his best friend. No penetration, just loads of caressing and cock and ball play. Both boys slid off to Paradise as incredible orgasms rocked their bodies.

Calming down, Tom couldn't keep his hands off Daniel's cock.

"This is incredible Dan, will you use it on me when we have some lubricant?"

"Oh God, yes, always."

That was scene set for some serious lovemaking when they got back to their house.

Chapter 2

When the boys arrived home from the stable they ran straight for Tom's suite and with no more to do, fell into bed. Tom kept a bottle of light lubricant in his drawer for when he masturbated. He withdrew it and showed it to Dan.

"I 'm going to make love to you before we go to sleep tonight, and I'm going to take a very long time to do it because I need to show you how much my love for you has grown over the last two years. First though, I want to play with you while you open me up and then I just want you to fuck me. I need to feel you inside me. I have for such a long time."

Dan was almost struck dumb. He had no idea that Tom had been in love with him for so long. He certainly wasn't reticent in his approach though. Tom was doing wonderful things to his cock and balls as he started to stroke a very cute butt before bringing slicked fingers into play to open up that little cavern of much anticipated pleasure. By the time he had four fingers fully embedded and rotating as they fucked, Dan was almost reaching overload. He had to get away from Tom's mouth so he swivelled round to get between his legs. The sight brought tears to his eyes, Tom looked so exquisite displayed as he was, he wondered how he could be so lucky. He bent Tom's legs to reveal his anus and then lubed them both. Supporting Tom's legs, very wide spread, he steered his rock hard cock to the entrance to Paradise. His glans slipped over Tom's sphincter and both boys exploded together with ferocious orgasms. Daniel fell forward onto Tom's chest and burst into tears.

"I'm sorry, I'm so sorry, I love you so much. Please don't hate me for ruining this first time."

Tom stroked the hair of this boy who he knew he would die for he had loved him so much for so long.

"What are you apologising for? That was so incredible, I may orgasm every time your fabulous cock passes over my sphincter."

Flexing his gluts and feeling that Daniel was still monstrously hard, Tom continued with laughter in his voice.

"Now, my little fuck bunny, do it again, and keep doing it until you can't get hard anymore."

Daniel pushed up to look into a pair of laughing and loving eyes. The kiss that followed would have curdled cream it was so hot.

"Oh Tom, I'll try never to let you down again."

Tom was still laughing, "You've never let me down, not now, and I'm sure, not ever."

The sparkle in both boys' eyes at dinner that night was too bright not to be noticed and Thomas asked what had made the boys so delighted.

They both lowered their heads and mumbled. Tom blushed a deep scarlet and Dan just looked terribly flustered.

Thomas wasn't stupid. Both of these boys were eighteen, very handsome with engaging personalities, but neither of them had ever been on a date.

"You won't have any problems in this house Tom, or you Daniel, but be careful outside, we would be devastated if either of you were ever hurt."

Tom looked at his father and saw the love and concern. In a whisper he replied.

"We will, Dad, and we'll still make you proud of us."

Thomas nodded and nothing else was said on the subject. It isn't necessary to make a big deal out of something you can't alter, and Thomas knew that at eighteen years old these boys knew their sexuality and nothing was going to change them.

The boys went to bed early and no one had any doubts why. They were very careful about their hygiene bathing each other but douching first. The erections were ignored with difficulty.

"I don't want anything to detract from the pleasure I intend visiting on you during the next two hours, Dan, so, much as I would like to take your nutrient, and vice versa you must wait until the right time."

Dan was tickled by Tom's concern that this lovemaking session should be perfect. Showing it by moving in close and giving him a kiss that made them both go weak at the knees.

Once they were comfortable with Daniel on his back and Tom lying alongside him propped up on one elbow, Tom started. Gentle caresses while he spoke.

"I think we still need to put some more weight on you Lover. You haven't got enough meat on your bones to cushion the shock if you ever have a fall."

Enough said, Tom took what he had and licked and kissed while speaking words of love to his new bed mate. The groin and anus took an inordinate amount of action before Tom eased over Dan's sphincter and took both of them to Paradise three times before he went soft.

"Your turn if you want it," Tom said with a grin as they lay alongside each other panting.

"I'm just going to empty my bowels of your love juice and clean us both up before I explore lala land."

Tom nodded, he didn't think he had the energy for anything else either. They slept curled up in each other's arms, discovered in that condition the next morning. All pretence of using the second bedroom disappeared over the next few months and Thomas decided to take further action.

The love these two boys had for each other just kept growing. It was obvious enough for Thomas and Charlotte to decide that Daniel ought to become a 'Sharp'.

For Tom and Daniel, that was the icing on the cake of their relationship. The fun part was that they now competed regularly, taking Red and Blue ribbons frequently

'Daniel and Thomas Sharp, have, once again, been awarded first and second place,' became a regular announcement at riding events. Their love and their prowess grew. Their loving in bed became breathtakingly satisfying.

The world was their oyster, everything they could wish for was theirs, until the eve of Tom's nineteenth birthday.

Thomas and Charlotte were flying back from Paris to be with their son on his birthday. The weather was marginal and Elstree had no instrument approach facilities. Thomas was informed and advised to divert to Heathrow or Stansted. He was impatient to get home and Elstree was closest and the home for the Beechcraft as well. He chose to make his approach to Elstree. The aircraft clipped the trees on final approach and cart wheeled into the ground killing both occupants.

Tom was devastated and it was left to Valerie and Dan to organise the funeral. The reading of the will had to be delayed until Tom was fit enough to join the world again. The loss of his parents had a devastating effect on him.

The estate was left jointly to the two boys, with Valerie as a lifelong adviser and consultant. Bequests were made to the usual people and staff were asked to remain with the boys if the boys wanted them.

It was nearly six months later that Tom sat a horse for the first time since the death of his parents, but the fire was dead. He didn't compete again being content to watch his lover who had saved his sanity. It was during one of these events that Tom came close to losing his mind. Daniel took a heavy fall. It was an awkward one falling at an odd angle. Medics realised how serious it was and special care was taken to remove him to hospital where x-rays showed he had broken his back.

"I'm sorry Mr. Sharp, but your brother is almost certainly going to be paralysed from the waist down."

The shock was too much for Tom, coming so soon after losing his parents. He left this world for somewhere else, somewhere that had no pain, no hurt, no pressure. He drifted. He had no idea how long he drifted, but it was nice here. He thought he would stay, until he heard a voice.

"Please Tom, come back to me. I'll live for you, but if you aren't with me I just want to die."

He thought the voice was familiar, it kept talking to him. The voice told him that it didn't really want to live in a wheelchair so if he didn't want to come back, that was alright and he would try to join him.

"Daniel', it had to be Daniel.

"Daniel, don't leave me, I'm coming back."

Daniel had undergone surgery as soon as the x-rays had been analysed. Vertebrae were seized where it was thought necessary so that no further damage could be done. Everything possible was done to make Daniel comfortable, but the end result was a paraplegic. He had normal functions and reactions throughout his body, except for his two legs. It was considered a possibility that with braces he would be able to walk with crutches, but nothing better than that was anticipated. To get him to this point took months. He spent as much of his day as he could sitting with Tom, holding his hand and telling him how much he was loved.

"Why is Tom in a coma Doctor?"

The only answer that could be given sounded ridiculous.

"Tom's brain shut down after he thought he had lost you. On top of the loss of his parents he wasn't strong enough mentally to lose you as well."

The idea of shutting down Tom's life support systems had been broached and turned down flat by Daniel, supported 100% by Valerie, who was now running the Sharp corporation.

Tom was twenty by the time he spoke those first words to Dan.

Doctors were summoned and stood round watching as Tom came out of his self-induced coma. The first clear view he had was of Daniel in a wheelchair, looking half the size of the Daniel he left. That was too much and the tears flowed freely before Tom slid back into unconsciousness.

Monitors were checked, readings taken and a big sigh from the lead consultant.

"It's alright, he's unconscious but still with us. I think he'll sleep for a while but be stronger when he re-joins us."

He was. The next time Tom woke he could see Daniel asleep in his wheelchair, a hand holding his own.

'He can't be comfortable sleeping like that, he should be in bed', was Tom's thought.

He saw the emergency button and hit it. The night nurse was in the door in a few seconds.

"Nurse, Daniel should be in bed, he is much too damaged to be sleeping like this."

"I think he may be glued to that chair Mr. Sharp. He hasn't left your bedside for months except for the bathroom. Nothing the staff here could do would move him. He is far too ill to be keeping this vigil and we have become very worried about him."

"Get some assistance and put him to bed." Tom looked at the bed next to his. "Why don't you move my cabinet out of the way and move my bed next to that one."

"We suggested that, but he didn't think that was close enough."

"Well he will now. We can talk about a big bed tomorrow."

Daniel woke slowly, picking up most of the conversation until he was fully awake.

"I'm not moving until you can move me."

"You don't have any choice. I'm going to look after you now, and the start is a proper bed. Tomorrow we'll get a larger one so that we can sleep together, but for now you'll still be able to hold my hand, but from your bed."

Daniel saw the determination, besides which, he really was tired and the chair wasn't comfortable.

Both boys slept until late in the morning. Doctors had taken all the readings they needed to breathe sighs of relief. These two young men were going to heal each other. The strength flowed through them as they lay there holding hands.

Tom woke and needed two things. A pee and a proper shower, the male nurse on duty took him for both. Daniel woke as soon as Tom moved and was assured he would be back.

The nurse was almost overcome by the sight of a vertical Tom. He was way beyond beautiful and appeared to ooze sweetness and light. Bathing him was breathtakingly erotic, but Tom just wallowed in the feel of the hot water coursing over his body.

Everyone was amazed at how well Tom was moving after more than six months in a coma. The physio boys had obviously done a grand job.

While Daniel was given a bed bath, Tom talked to Valerie and the lead consultant on Daniel's case. All Daniel needed to regain his strength was the will to do so. He was not in any danger now and exercise programmes were available to strengthen his upper body and to allow him to walk, once braces were fitted. Tom took it all in but couldn't hide the tears, knowing now that this boy that he loved was doomed to wheelchairs for the remainder of his life.

"Valerie, I want the house converted for wheelchair use immediately. Chair lift fitted, or a proper lift if possible. My bathroom to have all the necessary handholds, benches etc. fitted so that Daniel can be independent. All entrances to have ramps. I want a specially adapted car with easy wheelchair stowage. Consult experts, but no money is to be spared to make our home a place Daniel can feel normal in."

"It's in hand Tom, we haven't done anything up to now because Daniel was dying of a broken heart, not a broken back."

That statement made Tom sit up. "He what?"

"He was dying for love of you. If you hadn't come back to us we would have buried both of you together."

That statement shaped Tom's thinking for years.

Looking at Daniel each day was almost like looking at a blow-up doll as he regained his previous form. With his soul mate whole again, his appetite grew and he attacked his exercise programmes with enthusiasm not expected by his trainers after so many months, he quickly grew back to the Daniel Tom had known.

'I may be crippled but I am still going to be as good as I can be for Tom', was his guiding principle as both boys worked to bring themselves back to health. Their love for each other shone through every activity and amazed strangers.

They made a joke about introducing themselves as brothers, feeding off each other, making their humour contagious. There was that extra glow of bright light that appeared to follow them wherever they went, and for weeks that was the hospital.

Valerie needed so many papers signed for the estate to function that the reading of the will took place in the boys' room and Tom was immediately buried in paperwork, always telling Daniel what he was doing and what he was countersigning.

"I don't deserve any of this Tom. I'm just a stable boy that pleased you with his treatment of your horse."

Tom laughed. "Right, you're just a stable boy with a God given talent to ride and a personality that dragged me to you like a magnet. I know I would die without you so you are worth half of the Sharp Empire."

Dan loved it, Tom was the most beautiful thing that had ever happened to him. But, the sadness was there. He would never again see the Blue Ribbon tied to his horse's bridle. Tom saw the slow tears as they drifted down Daniel's face and knew, without asking.

"We'll work something out my love. Your world is my world, we'll build our new one together."

Chapter 3

The most difficult decision that Tom had to make concerned the horses. He thought he ought to sell them because he wouldn't ride without Daniel. Both were still quite young but he couldn't see them getting any use now. Daniel vetoed the sale.

"Please Tom, I know I can't ride, but you shouldn't give up. I know I will still love to see you ride even if I can't."

The horses remained but were seldom ridden by Tom. Valerie took charge of them unbeknown to Tom and Daniel. They competed frequently with other riders, Valerie always hoping that things would change for Daniel and the boys would ride again.

In bed, Daniel was frustrated, occasionally breaking down and sobbing in Tom's arms.

"It doesn't matter that you always have to be on the bottom Dan. Everything functions and, honestly, I love to ride your monster." He laughed. "Riding Eagle was never this exciting."

Tom could always make Dan smile, and yes, their lovemaking was still very good. It was exciting to 69 with him and then watch as he rode his cock. He would play with Tom's cock and balls while this was going on, and both always had wonderful orgasms. The frustration was because his legs were useless and he so wanted to make love to Tom properly like they used to.

Dan tried to get around as much as possible on his crutches. It proved difficult and he couldn't do it for long periods. He realised that Tom wasn't getting the exercise he should so he broached the idea of him joining a racket club of some kind, tennis or badminton.

Only a few miles from the house was a fitness centre and Tom asked about badminton clubs. He found out that there was an LGBT club that met on Sunday evenings. He decided to go along one Sunday, leaving Dan studying with Valerie.

"If you own half of this corporation, you might as well learn how it all works," was Tom's comment one day, so Dan had started learning from Valerie.

At twenty years old, and with his killer smile, Tom became an instant favourite with all the gay badminton players. Many made no secret of their desire for a closer relationship. His popularity climbed as his ability grew. He was always quiet and unassuming, told the other players little about his background, just saying that he lived with his brother. The showers had most of the players almost gagging when they saw Tom stripped. He used to have a drink with them afterwards, but continued to turn down invitations for dates.

It was about two months after he started playing that Tom did accept an invitation to a celebration party for one of the players after the game.

"Can I bring my brother along?"

Of course the answer was 'yes', they all wanted to know more about Tom.

When Tom turned up to play the following week Daniel accompanied him.

"Hi guys, I'd like you to meet my brother, Daniel."

Everybody looked so surprised that Tom and Dan creased up with laughter, but he took pity on them all. "When my parents realised how much I loved Dan, they decided to adopt him as he was an orphan. So, he's my brother, my lover and my best friend."

During the course of the evening they found out that Dan had fallen from a horse and ended up in a wheelchair. Watching the two boys interact with each other they all realised that there was no chance that Tom was about to fall into bed with any of them. Disappointment registered on several faces. Taking someone as gorgeous as Tom to bed was the stuff of dreams.

One of the badminton players was an orthopaedic surgeon and started to take an interest in Daniel from a professional view. He talked to the neurosurgeon who had confirmed the nerve damage at the time of the accident and made the recommended orthopaedic procedure to limit any further damage. During the next year advances in spinal surgery produced a by-pass system, enabling nerves to be spliced into a system to complete the circuit. The two surgeons got together and asked for Daniel to be brought in for an assessment. Many tests later the two men agreed that a further operation could be beneficial.

"No promises, but we won't make matters worse and could make them a whole lot better."

Dan was all for it, anything that might get him on his feet would be worth a try, Tom of course was worried that Dan's expectations might be too high and cause untold psychological damage if things didn't improve. They didn't. Both surgeons were mystified as to why Daniel still showed no feeling in his legs. Three months after the operation they opened him up again to have a look. Both men looked embarrassed when they saw what they had done wrong. A correction was made, Daniel was sealed up again and they waited. Twenty-four hours later, Dan squealed when a needle was pushed into his left leg, and again when it was done to his right one.

"Wriggle your toes Daniel."

So, he did.

"Bend your legs."

He did, with difficulty and some pain.

"I think a heavy course of physio and you will walk out of this hospital, Daniel without leg braces, but you will probably need crutches and sticks for a while."

Prediction correct and two of the happiest young men in the world walked out of the hospital a month later. Daniel had worked with his physio until he was exhausted, every day. Now, he could walk with just the use of sticks.

With his burgeoning mobility, Daniel's thoughts turned again to horses. He was intelligent enough to realise that jumping was probably not going to be on, but he could do dressage, which at least would get him on a horse. It was decided that Foxglove was young enough to train for this and Daniel started riding again. What Daniel did, Tom did. Both boys swamped Valerie with kisses for keeping the two Arabians and keeping them working. A third one was purchased for Tom to have a spare and he returned to eventing, swapping horses to keep them both in trim.

Tom decided that more centralisation of their lives was required so he built a new complex in the grounds of the house below the tennis courts. A complete stables with paddocks and a show arena where he and Daniel could practice. The arena had a small set of seating, all luxury Pullman chairs with tables in between and a small dispense bar at the side. A trainer/head groom was employed and the boys were in their element. Tom was going to make their money work for their enjoyment, and those of their friends.

The grand opening had been planned by Tom and Valerie without letting Daniel in on it. A few of the dressage riders were invited to an opening event, along with a few of Tom's eventing friends. Yes there would be winners, but Tom was going to give prizes to all participants. He invited all of the badminton crowd, and particularly the surgeons who had put Daniel together again. The judges on the day awarded Daniel a special commendation for third place in the face of his overcoming almost impossible odds to ride again. They wanted to award Tom the Blue ribbon but he told them that he was to come no higher than third however good he was. The badminton crowd was blown away with the wealth that was on display never realising that this self-effacing young man was so wealthy.

The party moved to the house after the riding and Tom turned it into a champagne celebration of Daniel's return to the show arena.

That night, despite a huge amount of champagne passing through them, Daniel made love to Tom properly for the first time in nearly two years.

It was almost necessary to issue a flood warning with all the happy tears shed that night.

Tom wasn't the only one who could be devious. On his thirtieth birthday, Daniel competed with Tom in a full eventing competition and took the Blue Ribbon with Tom taking the red. Like their first one when Daniel shed a bucket of tears, this time it was Tom's turn. To see his soul mate, his brother, his best friend and his lover compete successfully again over the jumps was more than he had ever dared hope for.

~~The End~~

Here is a sample from another story you may enjoy:

Dexter Chase

No Hoper

GAY EROTIC ROMANCE

"I don't think we can possibly do a worse job with this boy than we already have done so far, Mr. Turpin. So, despite being very unsure about placing a teenager with a gay foster couple we are going to let you have Daniel Harding. I'm surprised that after reading his notes you are even prepared to think about taking him never mind actually doing so."

"Your confidence in myself and Paul overwhelms me, Ms. Carpenter."

Tom had heaped so much sarcasm into that statement that Janet Carpenter had to laugh. "I'm sorry, Tom, but you know how my department views gay fostering."

Tom placed an arm around the petite lady and gave her a hug. "I know. You were a breath of spring when you took over from the witch. You know, Paul and I have so much to give to a kid and no way to do it unless we could foster."

"Well, for better or worse, I'll bring him round tomorrow morning. We have bought him two sets of new clothes because he came to us with nothing except what he was wearing, and that was a couple of sizes too big and probably a hand-me-down three or four times over. Your allowance for keeping him allows for a reasonable spend on clothes and pocket money. I hope you will actually spend it on the boy."

Tom looked hurt at that comment. He knew all about fosterers that just did it for the money, half-starving the kids and keeping them in rags, almost. "You know we would do this for nothing, Janet, so that comment was below the belt."

Janet blushed, "I'm sorry, Tom. I guess I'm getting cynical like the rest of my colleagues."

"Never mind, let's see if Paul and I can change your mindset a little with this one."

Janet left the house thinking, '*I hope so as well Tom, this boy is drawing on the last reserves of his strength to handle the abuse and starvation of his last homes, and the county facilities didn't prove much better for him.*'

*****

Paul Bright was Tom's partner. A very dedicated equal rights lawyer, who knew how much Tom wanted a kid to fuss over, but he was very dubious about this one. He had read the notes about the kid as well and realized he was going to take an awful lot of Tom's time and energy.

"He is arriving tomorrow morning, Lover, perfect timing. I sent the draft of my new book to my publisher this morning. I've mapped out my next one and can attack it in slow time. It won't matter very much if I don't do any work on it until the boy goes back to school."

Paul shook his head, he knew already that Tom had put in a load of work on the boy's bedroom and had shopped for new furniture for it, along with personal gear for the boy.

*****

The next morning at 10:00, Tom answered the door to be faced by Janet and a seventeen-year-old boy that looked about ten. He was so skinny and undernourished.

"Good morning, Tom, this is Daniel Harding. Daniel, meet Tom Turpin." A very frightened boy looked at Tom for a second before dropping his head to look at the floor and, in a very quiet voice mumbled, "Hello, Sir."

Tom looked at Janet and winced. This kid was trying to be invisible. "Hello, Daniel. Come on in."

The boy didn't move from Janet's side.

"I won't come in, Tom. I am already late for a meeting. I'll call in a few days to check if you are ok, but you have my number if you need me." Janet turned and left, leaving the boy on the doorstep with a back pack and nothing else.

"Come on then boy, let's get you settled in. We will have a busy week to get you really comfortable." Daniel moved into the hall, giving Tom as wide a berth as possible, noted by Tom. "Let's dump your gear and then we'll get started."

If you enjoyed this sample, look for **No Hoper**.

Also by this Author:

From the Author

If you enjoyed any of my books then please share the love and click like on my books in Amazon.

If you write me a review and send me an email I will send you a free book, or many.
(Just know that these emails are filtered by my publisher.)

Good news is always welcome.

One Last Thing, For Kindle Readers...

When you turn the page, Kindle will give you the opportunity to rate this book and share your thoughts on Facebook and Twitter. If you enjoyed my writings, would you please take a few seconds to let your friends know about it? Because... when they enjoy they will be grateful to you and so will I.

Thank You!

Dexter Chase
dexter_chase@awesomeauthors.org

About the Author

Dexter Chase is a writer of hot, gay erotica stories in both paperback and Kindle versions.

His very first book published is **Mastered (Sensual Tales from Ancient Egypt)** which is about an eighteen-year old Ajax, who was taken as a slave and brought to a great house by a high-ranking soldier.

Check out his books and you'll enjoy extreme gay erotica of all time.